It's
MY birthday!

PAT HUTCHINS

It's MY birthday!

Greenwillow Books, New York

Gouache paints were used for the full-color art.
The text type is Benguiat Book.

Printed in Hong Kong by South China Printing Company (1988) Ltd.
First Edition   10   9   8   7   6   5   4   3   2   1

Library of Congress Cataloging-in-Publication Data

Hutchins, Pat, (date)
It's my birthday! / by Pat Hutchins.
p.   cm.
Summary: Billy is reluctant to share his birthday presents
with the other little monsters, but then something
happens to make him change his mind.
ISBN 0-688-09663-8 (trade).   ISBN 0-688-09664-6 (lib. bdg.)
[1. Sharing—Fiction.   2. Birthdays—Fiction.
3. Gifts—Fiction.   4. Monsters—Fiction.]   I. Title.
PZ7.H96165It   1999   [E]—dc21
98-13379   CIP   AC

For Cathryn Morgan-Jones
(Hutchins)

It was Billy's birthday.

Grandma gave Billy a brand-new ball.
"Can we play with the ball, too?"
asked the other little monsters.
But Billy didn't want to share his new ball with anyone.
"No!" said Billy.
"It's MY birthday."

So the other little monsters played with a balloon.
And Billy played all on his own.

Grandpa gave Billy a brand-new jump rope.

"Can we play with the jump rope, too?"
asked the other little monsters.
But Billy didn't want to share
his new jump rope with anyone.
"No!" said Billy. "It's MY birthday."

So the other little monsters played with the ribbon.
And Billy played all on his own.

Ma and Pa gave Billy a brand-new red car.

"Can we play with the red car, too?"
asked the other little monsters.
But Billy didn't want to share his new red car with anyone.
"No!" said Billy. "It's MY birthday."

So the other little monsters took the empty box
and played with it together.
And Billy played all on his own.

Then Hazel gave Billy
a brand-new box of games
he couldn't play on his own.
"Can you play with me?" asked Billy.
"No!" said Hazel.

And she went out to play with the other little monsters and left Billy all alone.

"We'll play the games with you, Billy," said the other little monsters.

"Good," he said. "But first we'll play with my ball and my jump rope and my red car. It's MY birthday."

And they all played together.

When Billy's birthday cake came,
the other little monsters said,
"Blow your candle out, Billy,
It's YOUR birthday!"

So he did—

and he shared his cake with everyone.